DOWN ON
FRIENDLY ACRES

Fiddlesticks and gumdrop bars! Welcome to Down on Friendly Acres, a series based on the life of a real family—my family—the Friend family. My parents were farmers. They raised crops, livestock and me, along with my two brothers and sister, on a farm rightly named **Friendly Acres**.

I was raised on the farm in the 1950s and 1960s. Things were very different back then, and even more different when my parents and grandparents were little. From generation to generation the world around us constantly changes. Fashion changes, word meaning changes, technology changes, music changes, culture changes. One thing that remains constant is the need and desire for long-lasting, meaningful relationships—a family. Common threads that run through any family unit are the need for love, trust, encouragement and a sense of belonging. Along with positive emotions come worry, anxiety, and fear of people, places or things.

In this book you will find the Friend family experiencing emotions—good and bad. We don't always have control over those emotions, especially since emotions can appear in a blink of an eye. The good news is we have the opportunity to respond positively to those experiences. The bad news is we have a choice to respond negatively to those experiences. Every day we make choices. But in the end our choices make us.

We all face challenges. We all make choices. It's just a part of life. One day, if you haven't already, you may be asked this proverbial question, "Do you see your cup [representing your life] half empty or half filled?" What fills up your cup? Do you see the good news in life even in challenging situations? Or do you see bad news and wonder why your cup is not filled to overflowing? I know if my parents were alive today, they would challenge us all to look at life in good times and bad and choose to spill over with love, laughter and joy—even in moments of frustration, anxiety, worry and doubt.

Grandma Brombaugh, the undercover angel, was a prime example of living a life filled to overflowing with love, laughter and joy. Her sayings were as colorful as her cheerful dresses. Some of her poetic phrases puzzled me until I realized in researching this book they were actually generational popular expressions. Grandma used words like "heebie-jeebies," "horsefeathers" and "bee's knees." And of course, the undercover angel didn't want anyone saying bad words; so if something unexpected or bad happened to me—my response: "fiddlesticks and gumdrop bars!" Duane's choice of words was "cheesy pizza!" We can still be heard saying those same phrases today.

As you may know already, Down on Friendly Acres' cliffhangers are always based on true events. The soon-to-be resolved cliffhanger from the last book, Woolly Baaad Lies, is actually what happened in the middle of the night at Grandma's house. This family farm series continues mixing fiction with nonfiction, which in turn makes for some tall tales. Keep in mind that during this time in history most everyone owned only one phone—a rotary phone with a party line (and only five-digit phone numbers). Poodle skirts and penny loafers were popular. Daddy really owned a sulky, and a racehorse named Rosie.

Unfortunately for me, the roof fiasco and the running for my life incident are two things I'll never forget. And yes, I wanted to be like Duane when I grew up—still do. He was and is trustworthy.

Scared Silly Secret *started out just to be another true story about my brother and me camping out. The Friend family didn't even own a tent, let alone sleeping bags or camping equipment. We simply wanted to spend the night outside by ourselves. So we did. Daddy parked the cattle truck next to the house. I fell fast asleep but Duane kept seeing strange shadows and hearing weird noises. Unable to let him fall asleep, his imagination drove him crazy. That restlessness led him to wake me up out of a deep sleep, and our awesome anticipated adventure came to a disappointing end.*

But as life surprises would have it, there's more to this story. Combine an early morning hike that I took in the woods not too many years ago, and (in a blink of an eye) an unexpected encounter with nature, and the plot thickens. My choice was to turn that surprisingly scary moment into an unbelievable hair-raising adventure for you. My encounter in the woods indeed took place. Rest assured, I learned my lesson in the last book, Woolly Baaad Lies—*I'm telling you the truth and nothing but the truth.*

And last but not least: like all my cliffhangers, this book's cornfield conundrum really happened. But again, you'll have to wait for book number seven! **Fiddlesticks and gumdrop bars!**—*I've run out of room again. Remember,*

I'M A FRIEND
and U R 2!

R. Friend

DEDICATION

. . . to my precious husband, Bill, who walks alongside me for to reach children's hearts and minds with seeds of a different kind. There are no words in Noah Webster's dictionary to describe the courageous commitment, the enduring encouragement, the tremendous talents, the sacrifices, the tireless mundane hours of paperwork, the humility and the joy that my husband displays day after day. My dependable husband is a man of integrity whom I, along with many others, trust with every fiber of our being. It is no secret he is a devoted father and father-in-law to our incredible, talented children and the best G-Pops grandchildren could ever dream, wish, pray or hope for to be a part of their lives.

. . . to my fun-loving husband, who appears as the endearing Billy Bob the Bed Bug in this series. The Bed Bug says this in my book and Bill does it in real life: "I can be your friend, your cheerleader and your confidant," to which R. Friend replies, "Now that's a true friend."

. . . thanks for the past, present and future memorable, magical moments! It's no secret, you are the best thing that's ever happened to me! Here's to riding into many more sunsets with you by my side!

R. Friend

Scared Silly Secret

Down On
Friendly Acres
#6

SUNFLOWER SEEDS PRESS

ISBN 978-0-9830089-3-4 Paperback
ISBN 978-0-9830089-4-1 Hardcover

Text copyright © 2015 "R. Friend" Ronda Friend
Illustrations by Doug Jones
Graphic design by Julie Wanca Design

Library of Congress Control Number 2015910545

Printed in the U.S.A.
Sunflower Seeds Press

CONTENTS

The Friend Family

Duane, Ronda, Diane, and Ronald

CHAPTER 1

Midnight Mayhem!

Fiddlesticks and gumdrop bars!

How did Momma expect me to go back to bed?

I'd been left in the dark about the mysterious emergency phone call. And besides that, it was dark as dirt outside my window. I couldn't have fallen back to sleep if I counted one hundred thousand sheep.

After hearin' the front door slam shut, I perched myself with bended knees on the window seat in hopes I'd discover what in the world was goin' down. Only to further my curiosity, I spied taillights as our family car bolted out of the driveway. On tippy toes I snuck out of my bedroom hopin' my baby sister, *Miss Hawkephant*, wouldn't notice.

Lodged at the top of the stairs, I peeked between the banisters. Momma was still sittin' on the radiator talkin' on the phone. Emergency in progress made eavesdroppin' appropriate. And I wasn't the only one. Bumblebee in her hand, *Miss Hawkephant* perched on my shoulder. Silent sign given, I whispered, "Beee quiet!"

A gigantic hippo yawn reminded me it was the middle of the night. Ears tuned in and eyes fixed, we heard Momma keep repeatin' herself, fortunately fillin' in the blanks.

"Trust me, Mother. Everything will be fine. Harold is almost there. He'll take care of the situation."

"mbmblbmblbm"

"Yes, he left as soon as you called."

"mbmbmblbmbm"

"No, I'm not hanging up."

"mbmbmblbmbm"

"Yes, you've never pulled my leg."

"mbmbmblbmbm"

"No, you didn't wake up the children."

"mbmbmblbmbm"

"Yes, it's an emergency."

"mbmbmblbmbm"

"No, I'll not hang up until Harold has everything under control."

"mbmbmblbmbm"

"Yes, trust me. Everything will be just fine!"

"mbmbmblbmbm"

"No, Mother, you're not a baby!"

"mbmbmblbmbm"

"Yes, it's rare that you get the *heebie-jeebies*."

"mbmbmblbmbm"

"No, you're not a coward!"

"mbmbmblbmbm"

"Yes, undercover angels never lie. And you've never really been afraid—except..."

"mbmbmblbmbm"

Lightbulbs EXPLODED in my head.

Unable to contain myself, I shared my thoughts with Diane—breathin' only twice. (First breath.) "It's all comin' back to me. Yesterday Grandma told her potato salad story to help me realize how important it is to be honest. I asked Grandma, 'What happened to make you stop tellin' lies?' Then she said, 'When I was about your age, Mother and I made a giant batch of potato salad for a church picnic. A huge chunk disappeared from the middle of the bowl; I was *hungry*.' Thinkin' about bacon, I replied, 'Really hungry?'" (Second breath.) "Then she said, *'My stomach was growlin' like a bear comin' out of hibernation.* When Mother asked if I had been in the potato salad, my brain said "yes" and my lips said "no." I knew Mother knew. But I didn't have enough courage to confess. A half-hour later, she sent me to fetch more potatoes down in the dark cellar. I was scared to death of what I found there. Starin' right at me was a beady-eyed, dead...'"

Momma repositioned herself. Afraid she'd spot us, we froze. Eyes fixed on the downstairs dilemma, I whispered the rest of the story all the while prayin' Momma wouldn't notice we were *hawkephantin'*. Feelin' drowsy (either from the lack of sleep or oxygen), I felt another humongous hippo yawn come 'n' go. I whispered directly into Diane's ear, "I'm not lyin'. Trust me. There are only two things that give Grandma the *heebie-jeebies*."

"Wyin' does. Wat's da uffer fang?"

"You'll find out soon enough!"

Simultaneously, we hippo yawned. Why can't emergencies happen durin' the day? Imagination ran amok. What was takin' place at Grandma's house? Eyes closed, more exhausted than I thought, cockamamie visions of pandemonium floated in my head. Evidently I dozed off for a moment...or two...or three...

Instantly, a tap on my shoulder found me bright wide-eyed 'n' bushy-tailed. "Momma! As Grandma Brombaugh would say, you scared the *heebie-jeebies* out of me!"

"I told *you* to go to bed!"

"I'm scared. Is Grandma safe 'n' sound?"

Two big bear hugs later, Momma instructed me to follow her downstairs. I looked behind me—no Diane. I supposed *Miss Hawkephant* had flown the coop and gone back to bed. So it was a surprise to enter the kitchen and discover Diane, burrowed in Grandma's lap, holdin' on to *Bee Nice,* her bumblebee.

Trust me, it's not a real bumblebee. *Bee Nice's* wings spin when you pull it around on the floor. The *real angel* bought it for the *wannabe angel's* second birthday. It reminds us all to "Be happy! Be nice! Be good! Be patient! Be kind! Be honest!" Grandma believes a bee is a marvelous miracle because their wings are too small for their body. Aerodynamically makin' it impossible to fly. Yet they do! Good thing the bee doesn't know that. I like *Bee Nice*. But I *don't* like real bumblebees— beautiful to look at but not delightful to hold.

Where was I?

Oh, yeah! To calm Grandma down, Daddy held her shaky hands while pryin' the famous blue skillet from her grasp. Designed to prevent bed head, a nightcap of toilet paper was wound around the *undercover angel's* hair *again*. Clearin' his throat, Daddy attempted to maintain a straight face: "Edna, as an overcomer you have faced many challenges. Except your fear of..."

Interrupted by strange noises, Daddy exclaimed,

"Up in the sky, LOOK! It's a BIRD, it's a PLANE, it's..."

Duane, decked out in blue pajamas and a red cape, bolted from the blue, proclaimin',

"Here I come to save the day!"

"If it isn't Mighty Mouse!"

Daddy's joke didn't sit well with Grandma. With outstretched arms, Duane ran circles around the table then came to an abrupt halt. At attention, hands on his hips along with a puffed-out chest like a peacock, the superhero was ready to defend 'n' protect the undercover angel.

I overheard Daddy whisper to Duane: "Mighty Mouse is a great hero but under the circumstances Superman might be a better choice." Duane whispered back: "Point taken!" Then he shouted, "This looks like a job for Superman!"

"You're *too* late!" I added.

"I am?"

"Next time, Duane!" Daddy said, then refocused on Grandma. "Edna, to overcome your fear of God's tiny critters, why not let the 'rat' out of the bag?"

"*Horsefeathers*! I realize I shouldn't be afraid of a teeny, tiny..."

"Mouse!"

"Thank you, Ronda. I don't even like saying the word, especially after tonight's fiasco. I was counting my blessings, when the most terrifying shriek and shrill filled the air. I jumped from my bed, flipped on the light switch and saw the *you-know-what* scampering. Apparently my long, piercing scream frightened that *you-know-what*, too. I was in a frenzy. I flopped around like a fish on solid ground. Before I knew it, I'd stepped on the *you-know-what's* tail! It shrieked even more—and climbed up my nightgown. Horrors! The *heebie-jeebies* came on; I danced the jig until that *you-know-what* jiggled right off. Darting first to the kitchen to grab my skillet, I zoomed to the living room and grabbed the phone. I took refuge on the ottoman, called Jean, then waited for Harold to come to the rescue! How can a teeny, tiny *you-know-what* scare the living daylights out of me?"

Duane understood: "I know the feeling. Being stung by hornets really did a number on me. Now I'm scared of all flying things, except superheroes!"

"Duane, there's not a person in this world who isn't scared or afraid of something," Momma assured him.

"That teeny, tiny *you-know-what* made me feel like a coward. During the Depression, Franklin D. Roosevelt, our thirty-second president, stated, 'There's nothing to fear but fear itself.' He was right!"

"Does being scared make me a coward?"

Daddy said, "Not at all, Duane. Everyone faces fear, but we have a choice. We can run from fear or face our fears head on. Superman said it best, 'It's never as bad as it seems. You're much stronger than you think. Trust me. Superman.'"

"When I was afraid, I called on my family who I can always trust," Grandma said. "Nevertheless, here was my backup plan—my trusty famous blue skillet. If I had to, I'd..."

"Beeeee Bunny Foo Foo?"

Diane interjected.

We all giggled.

"Watching Harold take my broom and chase that little *you-know-what* right out of my house made me happy as a pup with two tails."

"Don't take this wrong, Edna, but I noticed the *you-know-what* was just as happy to get out of the house as you were to see him go!"

"You can say that again!"

"Don't take this wrong, Edna…"

"*Horsefeathers*, Harold! Seriously, what would I do without my family? You've proven time and time again to be trustworthy—or, as I like to say, worthy of my trust. Trust is earned, not given. Even in the dark, I can count on you!"

"Speaking of the dark," Momma spoke up, "it is dark. Time for bed, *again*!"

Sharin' secrets, Grandma and my brother got so close that a streamer of toilet paper, unbeknownst to Duane, stuck to the back of his head! Hands lifted, the *wannabe* superhero took to flight, shoutin', "Up, up and away!"

"Grandma, thought you didn't like people tellin' secrets."

"That wasn't a person, it was *Boy Superhero*!"

"A superhero wearin' a toilet paper cape!"

Grandma grinned. "This grandma's spending the night! Diane and *Bee Nice*, let's *fly* upstairs."

The *flyin' trio* flew. I walked.

CHAPTER 2

Heebie-Jeebies, Horsefeathers and Bee's Knees

"Wake up, sleepyhead. Grandma's fixing breakfast then we're off to the garden. I trust you to bring my garden basket and don't forget the pumpkin seeds on the back porch."

"Trust me, Momma. You can count on me!"

Fiddlesticks and gumdrop bars! I *had* forgotten Momma needed me but I didn't forget Daddy was takin' me fishin'. Anxious to start my day, I discovered Diane in her high chair wearin' an upside-down smile. Accordin' to Grandma, Diane had a case of the sulks. Grandma read from from Noah's book:

Sulk \'səlk\ *v :* to be moodily silent

Sulky \'səl-kē\ adj *:* sulking or given to spells of sulking

---

Diane continued sulkin'. Someone didn't get enough sleep!

Breakfast is always a treat when Grandma cooks. Today didn't disappoint: eggs cooked to perfection in her famous blue cast-iron skillet. I chuckled, "I'm glad you didn't *hafta* use your skillet last night! That mouse, I mean *you-know-what*, was lucky to escape!"

"Hush, Ronda! You'll ruin breakfast!"

Our appetites not affected, we sisters scarfed down cheese-scrambled eggs, crispy bacon, ice cold milk and buttered toast topped with honey. Speakin' of honey, "Grandma, you're the *'bee's knees'*! Did I use that word correctly?"

"Yes!" Ronald walked in and blurted out. "It's a neologism."

Diane, confused, asked, "Kneel on wat?"

"You silly goose!" Ronald winked, then flipped open Noah's book.

Diane still sulked.

Neologism \nē-'äl-ə-ˌjiz-əm\ *n :* a new word, usage, or expression

---

"The world of words is a captivating world. Grandma uses words like *'heebie-jeebies,'* *'horsefeathers'* and *'bee's knees'* because a famous cartoonist named Billy DeBeck made those words popular. DeBeck's most famous comic strip, *Barney Google,* was immensely popular in the 1920s and 1930s. Isn't that right, Grandma?"

"Ronald's one *Amazing Walking Encyclopedia*—absolutely correct. Your father's favorite character was Barney's racehorse, Spark Plug—the cutest, most comical horse!"

She had my full attention now: "I love horses! Maybe one day I can have my own Spark Plug!"

"Me, too! Me, too!" Diane insisted.

Momma responded, "Correct, Diane, you are two!" With raised eyebrows, a suspicious smile, and a double wink she added, "And, Ronda, you are a *spark plug*!"

"Focus, everyone, focus," Ronald continued. "Spark Plug became a merchandising phenomenon—just as big in American popular culture as Superman in the late 1930s. His cartoons contained original neologisms. They became buzzwords."

I interrupted, "Did someone say, 'Buzzzz?'", but Ronald ignored me, reading:

Heebie-jeebies \hē-bē-'jē-bēz\ *n*

[coined by Billy DeBeck] : jitters

"DeBeck, attributed with creating words that became household words, coined the word '*horsefeathers*,' meaning...."

"Nonsense! Horses don't have feathers!!!"

"Correct, Ronda." Ronald used Bee Nice and Diane to demonstrate. "'*Bee's knees*' means 'sweet.' Bees fly from flower to flower collecting nectar. The sweet substance sticks to the 'bee's knees'—meaning the sweetest!"

Even with sweet talk, Diane sulked.

But I was enthusiastic: "I've coined neologisms!"

"Like what?"

"*Enddle*: the middle of the end of a worm! Then there's *Miss Hawkephant* and *hafta*..."

"Those words would *hafta* make their way first into households, then into the dictionary," Ronald replied flippantly. "That won't ever happen."

"We'll *hafta* wait 'n' see!" I replied.

Stealin' what had been a dialogue, Ronald monologued: "As a newspaper cartoonist, DeBeck drew characters using scratchy lines, giant feet and bulb-like noses. In 1946 the National Cartoonist Award...

"Blah, blah, blah, blah, blah."

He talked 'n' talked 'n' talked about every cartoonist

listed in the *World Book Encyclopedia*. "...Everyone's favorite, Walt Disney, born in 1901, brought his first cartoon to life in 1928 with a Mickey Mouse film entitled *Steamboat Willie*. With the use of a soundtrack, Mickey talked! In...

"Blah, blah, blah, blah, blah."

Ronald talks *without* a soundtrack. Head droopin', Diane quit sulkin'. Ronald's speech knocked her out cold. Granted, Ronald was full of fascinatin' facts, but there came a point when I started prayin' that Spark Plug would show up, takin' *Mr. Know-It-All* for a ride into the sunset.

Prayers answered. Okay, Spark Plug didn't show; but Farmer Friend did. Daddy stepped in to go over tomorrow's chores, so it was Ronald's turn to listen. Tomorrow, Daddy would be at the livestock auction. It would be Ronald's first time plowin' solo; Daddy trusts *Mr. Know-It-All*!

After givin' Ronald his last-minute instructions, Daddy said, "Jean, whatchu got cooking in the kitchen?"

"Hopefully, a big mess of fish."

"Whatchu got boiling on the stove?"

"Hot water to make Jell-O for the three layer salad."

"Whatchu got baking in the oven?"

"Cornbread!"

"I love your cooking! But it's your loving that makes a house a home!"

Fiddlesticks and gumdrop bars! Was Daddy thinkin' what I was thinkin'? He whispered in my ear! Yes! Yes!! Yes!!! My parents exchanged goo-goo eyes and apparently another secret. Daddy winked and said, "More than one thing is soon to smell fishy around here!"

Yes, Yes, Yes

Momma winked at me. Need I remind Momma? Grandma doesn't like people whisperin' secrets in front of others. Daddy left, singin' like a lark in love, and took *Mr. Know-It-All* with him. Grandma grinned. "*Horsefeathers*, what mischief could Daddy and I get into? Besides, a wise undercover angel once taught me to beeee patient—you'll *hafta* wait 'n' see!"

Meanwhile, the *other bird* in the room woke up— happy this time. Diane, back to her sweet self, buzzed *Bee Nice* around the table while Grandma recited their poem.

Bee-Attitudes

Bee is a great buzzword—be good, be nice, be kind!
Be thoughtful, be helpful, be trustful, all the time!
Be bold, be brave, be busy as a bee,
Be loving, be humble—don't forget—be worry-free!
Be happy, be strong, be grateful by the way.
Be patient, be gracious, be forgiving—night and day.
Be caring, be friendly, at times be fancy free,
And keep in mind, it's impossible for a bee to be a bee!
A bee's body is too big for his wings to work just right,
But that bee has not a care as he lifts off into flight!
Sometimes the things we don't know help.
Listen, here's the clue,
That bee just made impossible—possible—so can you!

The phone rang once. Momma answered. We have a *party line*. If the phone rings twice in a row, it's not for us. I've picked up the phone to make a call only to hear total strangers talkin'. Who are they? Where do they live? Why call it a party line? I'm tempted to eavesdrop just to get to know the strangers so I could invite them over for a party. Then they'd be a friend of a Friend!

Momma was preoccupied so I watched the *angels* play. I want to be like Grandma Brombaugh when I grow up—sweet and disciplined. Momma tells people, "Mother has a routine: she wakes up, drinks a glass of water, eats a healthy breakfast, has her quiet time, takes a long walk for exercise, visits the sick and shut-ins, and eats three meals a day with no snacking in between. To her, sweets are for special occasions."

Conversation complete, Momma concluded, "Sounds sweet, Erta. Six it is!"

"What's sweet, Momma?"

"Tonight Uncle Robert, Aunt Erta, Bobby, Dennis, Karen, Uncle Herman, Aunt Pauline, Dean and Janie are coming to roast hotdogs and make *s'mores*!"

"I wuv s'mores!"

Grandma grinned. "My baby sister, Glenna, was in the Girl Scouts when s'mores became popular. Girls pleaded, 'Some more, please. Some more, please!' So s'mores started out as *Some More*. The first recipe appeared in *Tramping and Trailing with the Girl Scouts* in 1927."

"*S'mores* is a neologism," I concluded.

"Speaking of sweets, Jean, why don't we bake a pineapple upside-down cake at the campsite."

"*Horsefeathers*!" I retorted. Grandma must be kiddin' —bake at a campsite?

"All we need is a Dutch oven, a hole in the ground and hot coals."

"Impossible!" I declared.

"So are bees fwyin'!" Diane shouted, "But fey do!"

Grandma winked. "Trust me."

"I didn't believe it either, Ronda. But, I've seen it and trust it will happen again," Mother replied. "I'm off to the garden, meet you there!"

"Trust, trust, trust. I'll *hafta* see it to believe it!"

Grandma and Noah explained:

Trust \ˈtrəst\ *n* : assured reliance on the character, ability, strength, or truth of someone or something

v : to place confidence : depend (~in God) (~in luck)

Grandma gave an example, "I knew in my heart I could trust your father to rescue me. 'Trust' is what I call a heart word."

"We wuv hart worms?"

"We wuv you, Diane!" Grandma smiled. "Noah Webster once said, 'The heart should be cultivated with more assiduity than the head.'"

Ronda admitted, "I have no earthly idea what that means!"

"Simply put, *a great brain delights in facts and figures. But better yet, a great heart longs to know right from wrong and chooses right. Be wise, seek knowledge but run for your life towards wisdom.*"

"Grandma, you're so wise. What can I do to gain others' trust? As you know, I recently told some woolly baaad lies."

"Somebody once said, '*Never trust someone who lies to you and never lie to someone who trusts you.*' Time will tell if you can be worthy of someone's trust. I believe someone is counting on you!"

I dashed to the back porch, collected the garden gear and scurried outside shoutin',

"'Trust is earned, not given!'"

CHAPTER 3

Can of Worms!

A short sprint to the garden, and I presented Momma with everything she asked for as I ran in place. "In order for me to be trustworthy, I'm goin' to *hafta* prove myself to be worthy of trust!"

"Why are you running?"

"I'm runnin' towards wisdom."

"Great!" Momma chuckled. "Wisdom abounds in a garden."

I love dirt. Great dirt produces yummy vegetables, fruits and awesome gigantic worms. Normally girls are afraid of worms. Me, I love worms! Daddy counted on me to collect the biggest 'n' best for fishin'.

Knees planted, head bowed, eyes peeled, diggin' deep for worms, I began to feel somethin' crawlin' first on my head—then my neck—my shoulders—my arms—my everywhere!!!

Fiddlesticks and gumdrop bars!

Thinkin' this might be the *heebie-jeebies*, immediately I sprang up and discovered...

I had worms!!!

Hundreds of worms poured down like rain all over my body wigglin' every which way. Relentlessly attemptin' to brush them all off, I shut my eyes, did the Hokey Pokey and turned myself around 'n' around. What was this all about? Dizzy, I fell down. Unbelievably the most gigantic, enormous worm popped up in view—*Mr. World Book Worm Encyclopedia* himself. Empty bucket in tow, smilin' from ear to ear, Ronald chuckled, "One would say I opened a can of worms!"

What was I thinkin'? I love worms. Laughin' hysterically, Ronald, Momma and I collected worms for fishin' before they disappeared. I joked, "You know what Grandma Brombaugh always says, 'The early bird catches the worm'!"

We laughed some more. Normally I'd have been upset, Ronald interferin' with my one-on-one time with Momma, but *Mr. Know-It-All* began rattlin' off one fantastic fact after another about earthworms. Evidently, it takes one to know one.

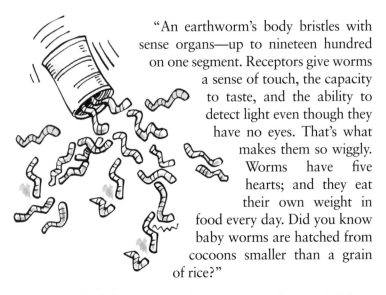

"An earthworm's body bristles with sense organs—up to nineteen hundred on one segment. Receptors give worms a sense of touch, the capacity to taste, and the ability to detect light even though they have no eyes. That's what makes them so wiggly. Worms have five hearts; and they eat their own weight in food every day. Did you know baby worms are hatched from cocoons smaller than a grain of rice?"

Ronald didn't give us time to answer. But, no I didn't.

"Like a miniature plow, worms squirm in the dirt munching their way through manure, soil, and decaying vegetation, producing worm castings with nutrient and organic matter levels much higher than that of the surrounding soil. Did you know their burrowing action helps to improve aeration, moisture retention and water penetration?"

Time's up again. Sometimes I wonder if he breathes.

Daddy and Duane (still sportin' the cape) walked by carryin' a humongous ladder.

"Daddy, don't forget—you're takin' me fishin'."

"It's a date! I'm counting on you to have everything together!"

"Trust me, I will!"

Great news!!!

Daddy needed Ronald. With Momma to myself again, I covered up a pumpkin seed. "Is this small seed afraid of the dark?"

"No. Plants are miracles that start as tiny seeds in the dark; then they sprout, breaking through the darkness. They bloom in the sunlight, then produce food. Your life started in the dark, too. No one saw you but we knew you were there. Day by day you grew inside my tummy. Children are miracles. Parents are given the responsibility to care for their children just like farmers are responsible to take care of their garden. If we're not careful, weeds take over. Farmers pull them so the good plants will thrive. Likewise, parents help their children determine between good seeds and weeds, or what I call..."

"...bad seeds! Like my woolly baaad lies' seeds that grew 'n' grew. Momma, I'm determined to plant seeds of a different kind—trust seeds. They'll take a while to bloom but I promise to prove I can be trustworthy."

"You're heart smart! When I was a little girl, your Grandma Brombaugh always said, 'One can buy seeds but one can't buy trust—trust is earned.' Earning trust requires learning from your mistakes. It takes time but it's well worth the wait!"

I thought, "Like mother, like daughter!" Momma enveloped me like a spider in a web as we spun a song.

L.eave A. M.ark B.ehind

Words and Music by
RONDA FRIEND

let - ting its light shine. Life's mys - ter - y,

once in dark - ness, ris - es to the sun.

It will die mak - ing seeds to sow, its work goes on and

life is short, help us choose what's right._____ And bloom where you're plant - ed, reap what you sow.____ In rain or in____ sun - shine,_____

42

43

Startled by a loud single applause we discovered Daddy, along with Teeny 'n' Tiny, eavesdroppin'. Eyes waterin', Daddy spoke softly, "People get too busy, taking day to day miracles for granted. May we farmers always count our blessings."

"Ruff, ruff, ruff, ruff!"

Daddy's head knowledge is dwarfed when compared to his huge heart. Wipin' his eyes with a handkerchief, he noted, "Looks like Teeny and Tiny are anxious to go fishing. Ready, Ronda?"

"Almost! I promise, these aren't secrets!" I said, before whisperin' first to Momma, "I'm plantin' trust seeds," then to Grandma, "I'm runnin' towards wisdom," and last to Daddy, "Everything for fishin' is on the back steps. I'll race you!"

Teeny and Tiny won.

Catch of the Day

Pretendin' to be a drill sergeant, Daddy shouted, "Fishing poles?"

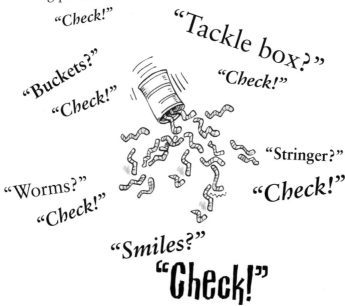

"Check!"

"Tackle box?"

"Check!"

"Buckets?"

"Check!"

"Worms?"

"Check!"

"Stringer?"

"Check!"

"Smiles?"

"Check!"

This soldier is one step closer to bein' worthy of her father's trust. Daddy told me that durin' World War II, drill sergeants marched their soldiers to different cadences. When troops needed somethin' to smile about, soldiers picked up the pace. In double march we sang,

"You get a line and I'll get a pole,
Honey, Honey,
You get a line and I'll get a pole,
Ba-abe, Ba-abe,
You get a line and I'll get a pole,
And we'll go down to the fishin' hole,
Honey, oh ple-ease be mine.
Go to your left, your right, your left,
Go to your left, your right, your left,
Hey!

Standin' tall and lookin' good,
Honey, Honey,
Standin' tall and lookin' good,
Ba-abe, Ba-abe,
Standin' tall and lookin' good,
We ought to march in Hollywood,
Honey, oh ple-ease be mine.
Go to your left, your right, your left,
Go to your left, your right, your left."

Daddy's name should be under the word "fun" in Noah's book.

Friendly Acres' pond has plenty of bullfrogs 'n' bluegill, some small mouth bass, catfish, and off to one side a half-sunken barrel. Fish love the barrel. And winters, when the pond freezes, Friends sit on it to lace ice skates.

"Daddy, city friends don't understand how I take a wiggly worm, find the *enddle* and place it on the hook without squirmin'. I explain to them that's what farm girls do. Besides, a girl's got to eat!'"

"Remember, Ronda, you invented the word *enddle*— the end of the worm and the middle of the end."

"Do you know *enddle* is my neologism?"

"No, I didn't, but now I do. Ronda, one is never too old to learn something new!"

Maybe I'll learn somethin' new and Daddy will trust me with his spinnin' reel. I've practiced castin' in the grass without a hook. Try as hard as one can, a line can get tangled with another line or snagged on submerged limbs or hooked on a rock. Daddy doesn't mind. I always trust him to fix my messes.

Right now, my cane pole did the trick. Bluegills were bitin' like crazy! To take them off the hook, Daddy taught me to hold them at the head then work my way down the back of the fish so their sharp gills won't cut me.

Takin' a break sittin' under the shade of a maple tree, Daddy announced, "Time for grass to sing!"

"That's impossible."

"Trust me."

Daddy picked out a strong, long, wide and not-too-thick blade of grass, then demonstrated. "With your right thumb and pointer finger, pinch the top of the blade; using your left thumb and pointer finger, pull the blade taut down the side of your right hand. Take your right middle finger and hold the bottom of the blade taut as you place your left thumb beside your right thumb. With the blade of grass stretched taut between your two thumbs, blow smack dab in the middle."

The impossible was possible! Grass sang! Music to our ears reminded us to work on our secret. Wouldn't be one if I told you!

Mission accomplished. We followed up with our cumulus cloud game. Imaginations went wild as we doled out names to cotton candy, puffy white clouds. "Look! Old Man Winter!" Daddy exclaimed.

"I spy a mustache!"

"I see a crocodile!"

"I spy a rabbit!"

"I see an elephant!"

"I spot two baby robins!"

That one threw me. "Where? There's not a cloud..."

Beneath a tree, he showed me two baby robins walkin' aimlessly on the ground. We interrupted our game to observe them.

Occasionally they jumped up 'n' down flappin' their tiny wings. Daddy pointed to their nest in the tree. Suddenly their sister fell to the ground.

"What happened, Daddy? She's on her own!"

"She may look like she's on her own but she's not alone."

"Where are her parents?"

"Momma's the one that gave her a nudge! Because parents love their babies, they'll let them fall. Fledglings flap their wings clumsily at first then repeat it time and time again until wing muscles develop. Soon the young birds realize unless wings flap, they'll never fly. Parents hang around just long enough to show them the ropes before they trust them to be on their own."

"Like Diane learnin' to walk," I added. "Holdin' on to my hand she'd take a few steps, laugh, then fall, hold on again, take a few steps, laugh then fall. Tryin' eventually turned into trust."

"We all fall. We all fail. But the more you try the more you can trust yourself to succeed. Speaking of trust, here's my rod and reel. Eventually trying turns into trust!"

Daddy trusted me. Fishin' from the shade of the tree, my longest cast ever landed the bobber perfectly positioned by the barrel. Waitin' for a bite, I quizzed Daddy, "Do you remember a racehorse named Spark Plug?"

"Do I!!!! I loved that comic strip character. I loved real racehorses, too. Robert and I were fascinated with harness horse racing. One day, Momma Friend trusted me to buy my own. I called her Rosie. That's when I bought a sulky."

"You can buy sulky? Diane was sulky this mornin' and I know she didn't buy it."

Daddy cracked up. "Sulky can mean that someone might be upset and prefers to be alone. Yet another definition of a sulky is a light two-wheel vehicle having a seat for the driver only. They're called 'sulkies' because the driver prefers to be alone."

"One's never too young to learn somethin' new!"

Daddy grinned. "My sulky is stored in the shed dangerously high on a wooden platform. You're too little to climb up that ladder or any...."

Zoned out, I envisioned the exact spot. It's very close to the rafters where the bats hang. I love worms but I'm not a fan of bats! Zoned in, I heard Daddy still talkin': "...then I sold Rosie. Your mother and I think it's time Friendly Acres had a horse."

Recallin' Momma's special wink, I jumped up 'n' down like a jack-in-the-box, shoutin',

"I'm gettin' a real live horse! Hi! Ho! Geronimo! I can't..."

Amid the celebration and without warnin', Daddy's pole was ripped from my hands. A huge catch on the line, the reel plopped on the ground headin' straight to the pond. Like a jackrabbit chased by a coyote, I ran, grabbed the reel and never let go. The fish didn't either.

Splish! Splash, Splish!

Losin' my footin', I joined the fish and bopped up 'n' down. Daddy, knee-deep in water, fixed my balance issues then instructed me to keep the tip of the pole towards the fish, and the line taut. A tug of war ensued. Eventually I won, reelin' in the biggest catch of the day—a small mouth bass. Then Daddy rescued me, drenched 'n' delighted, from the water. "If I had lost your spinnin' reel, I'd be sulky. But now I'm the happiest fishergirl in the whole wide world! Best part, you trusted me. I can't wait to catch me a horse, too!"

"Hold your horses, Ronda. It'll take time and patience finding the right horse. And it's still our secret!"

As I pulled my trusty clothespins out of my wet pocket and placed them on my nose, ears and mouth (girls *hafta* keep secrets somehow), I spied Duane runnin' towards us yellin', "Here I come to save the day!"

Duane came to rescue me.

Wrong! Soakin' wet 'n' wearin' clothespins, I gave him my "don't even ask" look. He gave me his "don't even care" look. Duane really came to catch fish. Daddy handed him the bucket. "Sorry, too late."

"Cheesy pizza! That's one big mess of fish! Let's eat!"

Since I was loaded down like a pack mule, one could say Duane did save the day. Partially wet, Daddy motioned soakin'-wet me to climb up on his back. Mounted, I shouted,

"Giddyup, Spark Plug! Giddyup!"

CHAPTER 5

Whatchu Got Cookin' in the Kitchen

Fiddlesticks and gumdrop bars! Fish stink. And I stank. After a quick shower in the basement, pleased as a cat with nine lives, I joined Lucky and the other cats to watch Daddy clean and fillet our catch. To show their appreciation for tasty scraps, the barn cats licked their paws and wiped their whiskers. They, along with Teeny and Tiny, were happy, happy, happy!

Momma, happy that Daddy showered promptly, cooked up a great lunch—pan-fried bluegill and bass, new potatoes, fresh green beans, three-layer Jell-O salad, coleslaw and cornbread.

"I love three-layered Jell-O salad. It's s-u-p-e-r!" exclaimed Duane, adorned in his cape. "How does liquid Jell-O turn into a solid?"

Before Ronald could begin, Momma wisely interrupted: "Another miracle taken for granted. By the way, tonight we're hosting a Friend cousin cookout and an overnight cousins' campout."

"And to top it off, the adults have planned a special surprise!" Daddy divulged. "Everyone needs to be on their best behavior. *Shenanigans* and *tomfoolery* should be kept to a minimum. In other words, don't do anything I wouldn't do!"

"That opens up another can of worms!" Momma smiled.

Diane asked who "Tom" was and why he was a "fool." Grandma winked, saying, "Someone that's quite familiar with the word should answer this question, Harold."

"Now Edna. *Tomfoolery*, also known as *shenanigans*, or pranks, is a secret, high-spirited behavior that can be fun for both sides if and only if both sides accept that it's okay to be on either side of the prank—the prankster or the 'prankstee'!"

"Wike when you twik us or pway jokes awn us?"

"Yes," Daddy nodded sheepishly. "That said, the boys will use Uncle Robert's army tent while the girls sleep in the cattle truck!"

"Do I get to camp out?"

"Ronda, time to spread your wings and fly!" Daddy winked.

"I don't wanna do vat," whined the half-bird. "I'd *beee* scared!"

"Diane, you can spend the night with me."

"Grammie! Me beee happy, happy, happy!"

I had two happy secrets. One I had to wait for *who-knows-when* to tell. The other one was about to be told, as Daddy grabbed his guitar and crooned, "I'm happy. My wife is one sweet, super-duper cook! Ronda and I did more than catch fish!"

Whatchu Got Cookin'

Words and Music by
RONDA FRIEND

lov - in'   that makes a house a home!

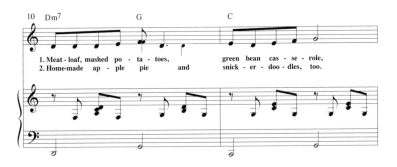

1. Meat - loaf, mashed po - ta - toes,   green bean cas - se - role,
2. Home-made ap - ple pie and   snick - er - doo - dles, too.

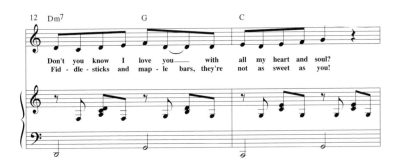

Don't you know I love you—— with all my heart and soul?
Fid - dle - sticks and map - le bars, they're not as sweet as you!

60

Fry me up some chick - en, ta - ter sal - ad, black - eyed peas, But
Dag - woods and root - beers, home - made ta - ter fries,

what I crave is hug - gin', so hug me pret - ty please.
My heart melts when I look in your

I love big brown goo - goo eyes. I love

what - chu got cook - in' in the kitch - en, I love ____

what - chu got boil - in' on the stove, I love ____

what - chu got bak - in' in the ov - en, But it's your

lov - in' that makes a house a home! 3. You're the

tang___ in my tart; ___ you're the choc-'late in my shake! I'm the
4. Take this with a grain of salt, as I chew on the fat, I'm as

bit - ter, you're the sweet— you're di - vine, my an - gel cake! I'm the
cool___ as a cu - cum - ber— our love is where it's at! I

64

39 E ⋯⋯ E/G♯ ⋯ Am ⋯ Am/C

pep - per, you're the salt; you're my pump - kin, I'm Cool Whip! I'm the

41 D7 ⋯ D/F♯ ⋯ G ⋯ G/B

flake in your pas - try— you're the hon - ey in my dew. You're the

43 D7 ⋯ G ⋯ F/G Em/G Dm/G

sweet in my tea; you're the cream in my brew!_____ I love—

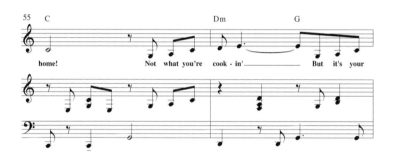

Speechless, Momma wore an expression that proved
hearts can *melt*.

CHAPTER 6

Run for Your Life!

"There's nothing I'd rather do than serenade my sweetheart, but there's work to do...

kitchen duty,

barn painting,

roof repairing,

hayride and bonfire preparations,"

...directed the drill sergeant.

"Move it, move it, MOVE IT!"

"Yes, sir!"
"Yes, sir!"
"Yes, sir!" we saluted.

When we had the kitchen spotless, Duane and I were sent to collect firewood and sticks to roast marshmallows and hotdogs on. My brother was to prepare the ground for the Dutch oven. Over the creek, down the long, long lane and to the woods we raced. Faster than a speedin' bullet, Duane had the advantage with his cape. He won. But I thought, "Just wait till I get my horse!"

Carvin' the last marshmallow skewer, Duane pointed his pocketknife to the pine tree's topmost point, where we admired the big nest. That nest cradles our local hawk. It's half the reason we nicknamed Diane *"Miss Hawkephant."* The other half comes from the word *"elephant."* If one of those shows up out here, I'll be runnin' for my life.

Imaginin' woodland creatures, I said, "Can you believe our parents trust us enough to spend the night in the woods *by ourselves? Aren't you afraid?*"

"Ronda's a scaredy cat! Ronda's a scaredy cat! Ronda's a..."

"I'm not a scaredy cat! I'm just sayin', 'lots of trees, lots of critters, in the dark might give me jitters!'"

"Critters like foxes, wood mice and skunks..."

"Oh, my!"

"Possums, raccoons and bats..."

"Oh, my!"

"Tree frogs, flying squirrels and spiders..."

"Oh, my!"

"Lions, tigers and bears!" Duane teased. "Got you, scaredy cat!"

"I'm not!"

"Yes, you are!"

"Am not!"

Still bickerin', we ran home. Exhausted 'n' hungry we stopped in the garden, pulled carrots and washed them off at the water hose. Hearin' the sound of the compressor on the other side of the barn, we moseyed over and discovered Daddy standin' on the second tier of scaffoldin', busy as a bee, spray paintin'.

On the first tier was the generator, creatin' quite a ruckus. Munchin' on our carrots we made eye contact. Daddy, arms wavin', seemed elated to see us. He hooted 'n' hollered, unfortunately to no avail. The generator racket drowned out his voice. So we moved closer. More excited to see us, he waved faster 'n' hollered louder! But his voice was just a rumble. Closin' in, we then heard,

"Run, run as fast as you can!"

So we did. The faster we ran, the faster he waved. Then it registered: his wave was not a *come-here* motion but a *go! get away!* motion. Daddy hollered, "Run, run *away* as fast as you can. There's some..."

Fiddlesticks and gumdrop bars!

Cheesy pizza!

Stoppin' on a dime, we glanced down and discovered a mess of bumblebees swarmin' from their nest. Immediately reversin' directions, we ran, pursued by bumblebees buzzin' our way—attemptin' to defend their home from predators. Meanin' us!

A bumblebee had stung Duane's right ear and lip, while another stung my right hand between my thumb and index finger. Droppin' our half-eaten carrots, we ran furiously.

Daddy caught up with us by the milk house. The trio, two of us with tears runnin' down our cheeks, burst into the house. My hand, swollen 'n' stiff as a board, paled in comparison to Duane's fate. It appeared as though a raspberry was attached to his lip. And his ear was "as big as a grapefruit," in Daddy's words! In my opinion, he exaggerated.

One would have thought Diane had gotten stung. Tears pourin' down her cheeks, she cried, "Momma, those bees need to change their attitude and *beeeeeee* nice!"

White as a ghost, Duane looked pathetic. Nevertheless a smile appeared. Flexin' his arm muscles, he boasted, "Look, man of steel! Only two stings compared to eight hornet stings last month at Grandpa Friend's farm. Look at it this way, they're *Superbugs*, defending and protecting their family. I'd have done the same."

Grinnin' from ear to ear, Nurse Momma fixed us right up.

CHAPTER 7

Two Rungs Don't Make It Right!

A scooter ride round the circle drive took my mind off the pain.

The two homemakers got in the car, about to head to Zuke's IGA Supermarket, the grocery store our neighbors, the Zukowitzes, own. Car window rolled down, Momma asked me to keep an eye on Diane, who was down for her afternoon nap. I dropped my scooter and hurried upstairs; I was eager to gain Momma's trust.

Grandma always says, "Practice makes perfect." Not today it didn't!

Duane, excused from roofwork, was recuperatin' in his bedroom. My brother's idea of recoverin'—ridiculous! Dreamin' of bein' in a band one day, he was playin' his saxophone. I reckon a big, fat lip is better than the alternative—worryin' 'n' breakin' out in hives like normal. It may calm him down but I was a wreck. Not only did my hand hurt, my ears hurt! As a beginner, he squeaks a lot.

Miraculously the full force of the floor fan drowned out both the squeaky saxophone hubbub and the hammers poundin' nails. Diane was sound asleep. Mission completed, I began plannin' the next. Who wouldn't love ice-cold lemonade on a hot summer day on the top of a scorchin' black shingled roof? The only homemaker left was me.

Thermos in tow, I made a beeline to the back of the house. Daddy and Ronald created quite a ruckus hammerin' the tiles. Addin' to the chaos, Duane's window was wide open right next to them. They didn't even notice Duane's squeaky serenade. Yellin' at the top of my lungs to "come 'n' get it" was useless.

Daddy's roofin' operation was quite involved. He had positioned a smaller ladder to reach the lower roof. At that roofline, a larger ladder led to yet another roof. I've climbed trees, I've climbed stairs, I've climbed hills but I've never climbed a ladder. I'd never think of climbin' that huge ladder in the shed. But what could go wrong with a baby ladder? Besides, Daddy's trustin' me more 'n' more. He trusted me with his rod 'n' reel, didn't he?

"Use both hands," I told myself, "everything will be just fine."

I was wrong.

One rung at a time, hand throbbin', I kept tellin' myself, "I'm strong!" Halfway up the ladder, my heart pittered-pattered. *Fiddlesticks and gumdrop bars!* I'd forgotten the thermos. I *hafta* go back.

Wrong again.

Climbin' up seemed a lot easier than climbin' down. Almost losin' my balance twice, I held on and somehow made it safely to the ground. Before I could think twice, I grabbed the thermos then headed back up.

Wrong, wrong, wrong!!!

Step by step, shakin' like a leaf, almost to the top, I looked down—not a great idea. The view scared me out of my wits; balance issues returned. The ladder moved. In slow motion, this tomboy slowly started fallin'.

Fiddlesticks and gumdrop bars!

"HELP! I'm FALLIN'! I'm FALLIN'!"

I missed a rung. Losin' my grip, I lost the thermos, which tumbled to the ground. Slippin' 'n' slidin' on several rungs scraped my bee-stung hand good and proper. In a tangled mess, hangin' on horizontally, injured hand poundin' in pain, I wrapped my left leg around one rung while my right foot dangled off another.

From the rooftop came a voice, "Two rungs don't make it right!" I looked up.

It was *Mr. Know-It-All*. Miraculously Daddy appeared alongside him and steadied the swayin' ladder. In desperation I yelled, "Grab my hand, Daddy! If you grab my hand you will never let me go!"

Daddy did, and didn't. Safe on solid ground, my father gave me the longest, strongest hug and kept sayin', "I love you, I love you, I love you. Thank God, angels were watching over my angel."

I kept sayin', "I'm sorry. I'm sorry, I'm sorry," all the while knowin' I'd made a terrible choice. I just knew I was in

T-R-O-U-B-L-E

F-O-R-E-V-E-R!!!

But I wasn't.

Surely he'll put me in time-out.

But he didn't.

Instead, he just hugged me. From the roof came a voice *again*,

"Able to leap tall buildings in a single bound!"

Evidently, hearin' my cries for help, Duane had crawled out his window to get Daddy's attention. Boy *Superhero* swiftly descended the ladder, ran circles around me and declared, "Here I came to save the day! And this time I wasn't late!"

Okay, brothers aren't all bad. As I swallowed my pride and thanked him, I couldn't help but notice Duane's ear had gotten bigger 'n' bigger. Plus, his lip had swollen to twice the size. Someone needs to keep an eye on him— OH, no! In all this commotion, I had forgotten to keep an eye on Diane.

I ran to her room. Good news! She was still asleep.

Upset with myself, I sent myself to time-out and rewrote the perfect "If life gives you lemons, make lemonade" song. Who knows better than Santa!

Up on the rooftop Ronda climbs
Up the ladder her very first time.
Scared and shaky—nervous too!
Knowin' it's something she shouldn't do.

No, no, no, Ronda shouldn't go,
No, no, no, deep down she knows.
Up on the rooftop—bing, bang, bong,
Knowin' all along she was in the wrong!

First comes the teeter and then the totter,
Add a shrill 'n' a shout—a hoot 'n' a holler.
Losin' her balance, Duane hears her call.
In the nick of time Daddy breaks her fall!

No, no, no, Ronda shouldn't go,
No, no, no, deep down she knows.
Up on the rooftop—bing, bang, bong,
Knowin' all along she was in the wrong!

Ronda's taught a lesson—trust and obey.
Parents know best—let them show the way.
They're all grown up—wise, protective, strong.
The more you trust—the less you're wrong!

Yes, yes, yes—Ronda, now you know,
Yes, yes, yes, when parents say no.
Climbin' up the rungs was wrong—not right,
Always trust your parents—they have foresight!

81

Unbeknownst to me, Daddy had been eavesdroppin'. He complimented me on the song and lesson learned: "We all make mistakes and poor choices. The best thing that comes from poor choices is to not make them again. As a father, I'm thankful that when I'm not around, Someone bigger than me is watching you."

The homemakers pulled in the driveway. Daddy told me to stay inside. Momma's about to hear about my *"rung"* doin'! Will they trust me enough now to spend the night in the woods? Time will tell.

Time's up. While bandagin' my hand, I informed Momma it looked worse than it felt. She instructed me to close my eyes, then she placed somethin' in my left hand. Sense of touch told me it was a small coin—not a silver dollar or a quarter, and it wasn't thin or small enough to be a dime. Process of elimination—I guessed, "A penny?"

"That's right! Keep your eyes closed. What's written on it?"

"*Horsefeathers!* It's dark. You tell me!"

"Okay. 'In God We Trust.' Now, Ronda, what's written on it?"

Bewildered, I replied, "In God We Trust."

"How did you know that?"

"You told me."

"How did you know I'm telling you the truth?"

"Because my parents *always* tell the truth. Even in the dark, I can trust you."

Eyes opened, I listened to Daddy explain, "In 1863 (during the Civil War), the United States Congress passed a resolution requiring several coins to be inscribed with the words 'In God We Trust.' Five years ago, in 1956, Congress passed a law, approved by President Dwight D. Eisenhower, declaring 'In God We Trust' as the national motto. That motto is inscribed on our coins and paper currency. We believe we can always trust God. He wants you to trust us, and you need to be trusted, too. It's difficult to let you try things on your own, but like robins, we all start somewhere. Besides, we can tell you are remorseful."

Remorseful sounded bad, but by the look on their faces it must be good. Momma simplified it. "The word 'remorse' comes from the Latin verb *remordere* meaning 'to bite again.' If bitten over and over again, one should learn her lesson. It boils down to feeling very sorry for having done something wrong."

"I am. 'Bitten' more than once, Duane and I've learned to leave a bees' nest alone! And after almost fallin' off a ladder, doin' somethin' I know in my heart I shouldn't have tried in the first place, I know now never to try somethin' new without permission."

"It's settled. We believe you can be trusted. Camping it is!" Daddy confirmed. "Keep this penny as a reminder, Someone always has their eyes on you."

I love my parents!

CHAPTER 8

Flyin' Purple People Eater!

The Friends' jaws dropped as Duane, draped in a cape, flew out of the house to greet them. By now his ear really was as big as a grapefruit and his lip had doubled in size. Aunt Erta thought I was wearin' a boxin' glove. Momma admitted goin' overboard protectin' my injured hand from infection.

With a full moon slated for this evenin', the weather was picture perfect. It appeared that we were spendin' a week—not just one night—as everyone piled beddin', stuffed animals, flashlights, coolers, and other supplies into the truck. Uncle Robert helped Uncle Herman load a large trunk. Cousins, curious of its contents, inquired but we were quickly warned, "For us to know and you to find out!"

Instructed to stay seated on the bales, we were all set. Daddy drove the tractor, hitched to the wagon, down the windin' lane. Uncle Robert followed in the truck. In anticipation of a fun-packed evenin', this rowdy group of Friends made their way over the creek and into the woods singin', "She'll Be Comin' Round the Mountain." There are no mountains on Friendly Acres, just cornfields, hayfields, pasture and woods. But with my eyes closed, I dreamt one day I'd be ridin' one sweet horse.

Yee-haw!

Lickety-split, camp was set. Entertained by the campfire's sizzlin' pops, whisperin' hisses and the smell of smoke and pine needles, cousins carefully custom-roasted their hotdogs. Momma commended Duane on the well-carved sticks and the perfect spot for the Dutch oven. "We can always trust you."

Cousins gathered around as Grandma, wearin' oversized leather padded gloves, turned the hot cast-iron kettle over, revealin' another take-for-granted miracle—a picture perfect pineapple upside-down cake. She and I exchanged winks as I gave her two thumbs up. Then our parents suddenly vanished as Grandma directed us to take a seat.

As the campfire blaze illuminated the bandwagon stage, we were instructed to close our eyes. Adult chuckles, snickers and giggles ensued, signalin' their special surprise was soon to be revealed. Shouts of

"One, two, three, four!"

accompanied by drums and cymbals made way for this evening's entertainment.

Eyes wide open, the older cousins roared with laughter; the younger cousins were bug-eyed and speechless. Diane started cryin'. To calm her, Karen picked her up.

Daddy, dressed from head to toe in a comical but somewhat scary purple outfit (thus the *Hawkephant's* tears), was the lead singer. An old tobacco lath became a microphone as he belted out "One-Eyed, One-Horned Flyin' Purple People Eater." Uncle Herman, out of control, banged furiously on the drums while Uncle Robert jumped up 'n' down, wildly strummin' the lead guitar.

The mommas, dressed in polo shirts, poodle skirts, crinoline petticoats, oxford saddles, and cat-eyed glasses, sang backup. They stole the show.

The concert was comical, crazy, scary and spectacular all rolled up into one. Even Diane loved it, once she realized it was Daddy in the silly outfit and not a monster.

Friends sure know how to party! Risin' to our feet, rhythmically clappin', we chanted,

"We-want-more!We-want-more..."

The undercover angel shot us her *mind-your-manners look*. Instantly our tune changed:

"More, please! More, please! More, please!"

The band obliged and sang a real toe stomper—"Who Put the Bomp (In the Bomp, Bomp, Bomp)." Another rousin' standin' ovation; we chanted,

"Some More, Please! Some..."

"S'mores?" Daddy questioned. "S'mores—coming right up!"

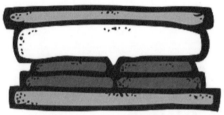

Those ooey-gooey treats are scrumptiously delicious! Ronald informed us that in 1829, Dr. Sylvester Graham, nicknamed "Dr. Sawdust," was concerned about people's overindulgence in sweets. So he invented the coarse, yeast-free brown bread with just a pinch of honey that became known as the graham cracker. He remarked, "Dr. Graham would roll over in his grave if he knew his healthy cracker became the bread for one of the most fattening concoctions ever."

Grandma added, "But like my parents said, 'Everything in moderation.' Why not enjoy a little sweet now and then?"

So we had some more s'mores! Except for Grandma. Remember, she doesn't snack.

The night couldn't get any better. Until we looked up. The crystal clear sky filled with twinkle lights and a full moon provided the perfect backdrop for nature's concert—an army of amphibian tree frogs croakin', the cicada chorus chirpin' 'n' clickin', and an owl hootin',

"WHO cooks for you, WHO cooks for you, WHO-o-o cooks for you all?"

Minus his costume, Daddy hooted his owl impersonation. "Jean cooks for me, Jean cooks for you, Jean cooks for you all!" he bellowed.

Leadin' us away from the campfire then, he pointed upward, "The North Star lies almost exactly above the earth's axis and is like the hub of a wheel. It doesn't rise or set. On a clear evening during World War II, I would spot it and smile, trusting it like a compass. Look! There's the Little Dipper and the Big Dipper!"

Face aglow, Diane sang, "Wike a dimeman in the sky!"

"You're my diamond, Diane!" Daddy told her. "You're all stars, you brighten our days and *now* our nights." To the group he said, "Everyone's eyes closed. Hold out your hands."

Eyes not completely shut, I noticed Ronald had disappeared. What shenanigans was he up to? Meanwhile, the cousins, each receivin' a wintergreen mint, opened our eyes. We formed a huddle and Daddy covered us in a huge quilt. Under the quilt's total darkness, he placed a mint in his mouth, began crunchin' it, and between crunches opened his jaws.

Amazingly, sparks flew like tiny stars in his mouth. One by one Friends took turns under the big top. Ronald returned just in time to create a sparklin' star galaxy in his mouth.

The memorable, magical moment night wasn't over yet. While the adults gathered their belongings, Daddy, with a suspicious wink, put Ronald in charge, warnin', "The apple doesn't fall far from the tree. So Friend cousins, don't overdo the tomfoolery tonight. And don't forget to hit the hay!"

Secretively placin' somethin' in my hand, Daddy whispered, "I'm counting on you. Trust your brothers and the Man upstairs to take real good care of you."

Addin' another shiny penny to my pocket, I saluted. "Yes, sir!"

Wagons ho! We waved. Discoverin' Grandma's gloves left behind, I grabbed them. Now the undercover angel can trust me to look after her. One last wave revealed Diane had already fallen asleep in Momma's arms. It was past her bedtime, but not ours!

Time for some Tom!

CHAPTER 9

Pranks for the Memories

Expectin' the cousin campout to involve more shenanigans, I was surprised when the boys just started gatherin' up the longest, strongest marshmallow sticks, then ventured off to the pond to go frog-giggin'. Ronald told us not to wait up.

Don't mind catchin' frogs by hand, but spearin' them with gigs—not my idea of fun. Informed we'd be havin' frog legs for breakfast, I decided right then 'n' there I'd be skippin' breakfast.

The "sweet" smell of *eau de manure* filled the air as we girls set up house in the cattle truck. I had brought my trusty clothespins and my red bandana, in case the stench was unbearable. Turnin' on her flashlight, Karen drew the huge white sheets Momma had hung as privacy curtains. We donned PJs, robes 'n' slippers, and gathered our stuffed animals.

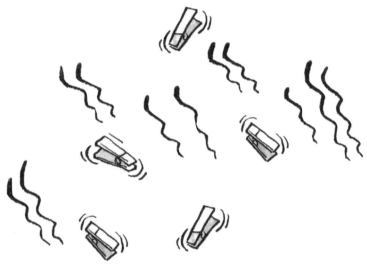

I tucked my pennies away in my pajama pocket, and Janie gathered my hair into a ponytail comin' right out the top of my head: like the cartoon character Pebbles in *The Flintstones*. Karen planned on sleepin' in her hairdo she came with—Pippy Longstockin' style—a little too uncomfortable for my taste. My jaw dropped as I watched Janie slap on globs of green, sticky, gooey Dippity Do to her mop, creatin' multiple twists, curls, waves and spirals stickin' every which way.

Karen had brought Pit, a not-so-quiet card game involvin' yellin'—right up our alley! More light needed, we switched on more flashlights. **Fiddlesticks and gumdrop bars!**

SPOOKY, EERIE,
mysterious,
and somewhat
CrAzy

shadows popped up on the curtain. Scared to death, we three jumped up in unison with a case of the *heebie-jeebies*. Realizin' it was just our shadows, we laughed uncontrollably; we were havin' way more fun than the boys.

Until we heard howlin'—strange howlin'! Switchin' flashlights off, we sat frozen in the dark. Hearts pounded:

Pointer finger flush to her lips, Janie whispered to Karen. This duo was up to no good—and I was about to join them. Unnatural coyote howls were comin' from every direction as Karen lifted the corner of the curtain. The howlin' sound turned into more of a "howl-ha-ha, howl-ha-ha" and an occasional "ribbit-ribbit." The full moon's light revealed tomfoolery was about to begin.

Surrounded not by coyotes but five *broyotes*, we knew our conspirin' brothers were sneakin' around pretendin' to be predators with hopes that we'd be scared silly. Karen whispered that Ronald was wearin' Daddy's costume, which explained his sneak away durin' the wintergreen mint light-up! Janie had the perfect strategy to counteract this planned prank. How we pulled it off? I don't know, but someone was about to get the *heebie-jeebies*. And it wasn't us!

With a little imagination and lots of creativity, we quietly donned our makeshift warfare costumes. As howlin' broyote predators prepared to attack our territory, Janie gave us the "Go!" signal.

Lights, action, CAMERA!

Instantly, the shadows of three girls and a few additional props created the scariest, spookiest scene imaginable. Bodies frozen in position, we moved only our eyes: in order to watch the predators' prank backfire. The one-eyed, one-horned flyin' purple people eater and the rest of the broyotes, scared witless, tossed their bullfrogs in the air, bumpin' into one another repeatedly in chaos.

Laughin' hysterically, we watched the terrified broyotes run in circles—with dozens of frightened frogs jumpin' out of their pants pockets, attemptin' to escape the fiasco as well. Defeated, daunted and eventually frogless, they ran to their tent for safety.

Giggin' was a deliberate decoy to distract from their desired devious deeds. Knowin' they had been made, the broyotes formed a pyramid as they popped their heads out of the tent. Defeat declared, they warned us they intended to return the favor someday! But it wouldn't be tonight. Worn out, everyone fell asleep.

That is, almost everyone.

Sleepin' like a baby, I was woken by a tap on my shoulder. My heart missed a beat. But thankfully a familiar voice whispered, "Help me, Ronda! Help, help me Ronda!"

(I still think that would make a great song one day.) Duane hadn't slept a wink. Minus his cape and breathin' down my neck, he explained, "My imagination is working overtime!

"Lying awake, I was hearing all kinds of sounds,

Aren't boys *supposed* to be brave and fearless? I dared not wake up the boys. They'd call me names. Wake up Janie and Karen? They're sleeping like logs. Cheesy pizza, I need you—you're my sister!"

Pleasantly surprised, I thought, Boy Superhero needs me? *Fiddlesticks and gumdrop bars!*

Jolted by another round of strange sounds, we held our breath till they subsided. Cautiously, I whispered, "Why do you need me?"

"My cape has disappeared. I need it."

"Like Linus needs his blanket in the comic strip *Peanuts*?"

"Kind of, will you help?"

"Actually, I'm honored you asked. You scared?"

"Remember, 'There's nothing to fear but fear itself'! Plus, between my fat lip and grapefruit ear and your boxing glove and crazy hairdo, if there is something out there, *they* will be scared of us first."

"This is a job for Siblin' Superheroes! 'Here we come to save the day!' Duane, you go first!"

Bob-white

screech

choo-choo

eek eek eek

peeper ribbit

OooLULLU

Hoo Hoo Hoo
Hoo Hoo Hoo
hooooo-ah

hiss, squeal, screech, whine,
whimper, stomp

chirp

whinny

Katydid, katy-didn't

whoop-whoop   skreek

Whip-poor-will

Tseep   ow wow wOw wow

Fowl Play

Fog set in. Flashlights on, shadows lurked everywhere and so did mysterious sounds. To calm our fears Duane and I played a guessin' game, namin' the animal sounds.

Not a good idea. Changin' tactics, we concentrated on backtrackin' the broyotes' steps in hopes of findin' the cape. After a backward glance to make sure we weren't bein' followed, I heard a thump followed by the breakin' of branches. Lookin' again, I found Duane had fallen flat on his face. Rubbin' his head, he rose cautiously to his feet. He shook his fist, and with a controlled whisper he uncontrollably yelled, "*Cheesy pizza*! Why did you hit me?"

Shocked, I *whispellin'* right back (my new neologism—a whisperin' yell), "What? I didn't hit you!"

"Yes, you did!"

"No, I didn't!"

"Yes, you did!"

"No, I didn't!"

"Well then, who did?"

"Whatever!" I continued *whispellin'*. "We're here to find your cape. Follow me!"

Enveloped in fog, and grateful for the worn path to the pond, I took the lead. A bizarre sound from behind struck fear in us both, but before I had a chance to turn around somethin' hit me on the head. For a split second, I felt a tug on my ponytail. Balance issues, I fell facedown, hit the ground and twisted my ankle. Motionless for several moments, I slowly stood up holdin' my ankle, turned, and *whispelled* even louder, "Duane Hamilton Friend, look me in the eye and tell me you didn't hit me on the head."

"I didn't hit you on the head!"

"You lie!"

"I'm not lying! I heard the commotion, turned to see where it was coming from, then saw you collapsed like a heap."

"I'm lyin' on the ground just as sure as you are lyin' like a rug!"

"I, Duane Hamilton Friend, being of sound mind, did not—I repeat, did not hit you over the head!"

"Yes, you did!"

"No, I didn't!"

"Yes, you did!"

"No, I didn't!!!"

"Look, you not only hit me on the head you messed my Pebbles ponytail up. It's a tangled mess!

"Your hair is a mess but I didn't do it!"

"Well, then who did?"

Ankle still sore, I let Duane take the lead. Frustrated, yet on a mission, we persisted. In unison we rhythmically repeated, "Things are never as bad as they seem, oh my! You are stronger than you think! Trust me. Things are never as bad as..."

Determination set in as Duane flew through the fog even without his cape. I lost sight of him in the murk. Moments later—another thud. Feverishly focusin' my flashlight towards the crash, I found Duane sprawled out on the ground like a sack of potatoes.

"How will we ever find your cape if you keep fallin' down?"

Standin' up, cape in hand, Duane was visibly shaken.

"You found it!" I cheered.

Duane seemed agitated. "I accidentally fell on it when you purposely hit me. How in the world did you hit me with such force without making a sound?"

"It wasn't me! I promise. How do I know it wasn't you hittin' me earlier?"

"*Cheesy pizza*! I'm your brother, trust me, it wasn't me!"

That made perfect sense. Duane's the one who had asked for my trust, so why shouldn't I trust him? Besides, Momma does. I secured his cape around his neck, and cautiously limped back toward camp. Duane followed.

Too close for comfort we heard,

"WHO cooks for you, WHO cooks for you, WHO-o-o cooks for you all?"

An instant chill ran down my spine. It wasn't Daddy this time! Before I could say *fiddlesticks and gumdrop bars*, I heard Duane shout,

"Up, up and away!"

Faster than a speedin' bullet, more powerful than a locomotive, arms outstretched, Duane leaped in the air— knockin' me to the ground.

I've had it with him. Attemptin' to stand, I got yanked back down, Duane shieldin' me with his cape and recitin',

"Things are never as bad as they seem, you're stronger than you think. Trust me, Ronda, I've got you."

Talons ready, a four-foot-wide feathered fowl skimmed right over our heads, barely missin' us both. Then, spread-eagled on the floor of the woods, it dawned on me. Duane had toppled me purposely, to defend 'n' protect his sister. Petrified, we slowly turned our heads and engaged in a staredown with a set of stunnin', soulful dark brown eyes. Perchin' on the ground five feet away, this proud creature appeared keenly aware of his surroundings. Without a sound he quickly 'n' quietly rose upwards on his powerful brown wings, roosted in a tree, and continued starin' down at us like unwanted guests. Duane *whispelled*,

"It's an Owl Fowl— a barred owl to be exact!"

Bodies shakin', unable to stand up to our predator, we sensed the fowl wasn't our only fearless foe. Hearts poundin', we apprehended the poundin' of footsteps nearin' us from the direction of camp. We were pinned in the middle. Soon it emerged from the fog: a one-eyed, one-horned flyin' purple people eater rushin' towards us! Its call:

"Here I come to save the day!"

The beautifully mottled barred owl took one look at the one-eyed, one-horned flyin' purple people eater, better known as Ronald, and silently winged its way into the fog, never lookin' back. Overjoyed as never before to see my big brother, I knew Daddy was right. Trust your family.

Funny thing was, Ronald apologized for bein' late. He had noted the owl followin' us as we were leavin' camp. He thought his best defense was the costume; but a few leftover frogs had taken up residence. That raised a campsite commotion. Mystery solved.

Duane and I had been distracted by all that noise. Ronald knew we wouldn't hear the owl, since, "Barred owls are silent predators capable of flying just inches from their prey without being detected—soaring through the air in virtual silence. The quietness of their flight...

"Blah, blah, blah, blah, blah."

Worn to a frazzle, up way past bedtime, I begged, "Enough, Ronald, that explains everything!"

Proud to be their sister, I locked arms with my superheroes. Battered 'n' bruised and definitely a sight for sore eyes, we traipsed through the woods chantin',

"Things are never as bad as they seem, oh my! You are stronger than you think! Trust me. Things are..."

Back at camp, exhausted, we bedded down for the night.

Hours later, fog disappeared as the sun peeked through the slats of the truck. Campfire blazin', bacon sizzlin', cousins began wakin' up to a cry of "Who cooks for you, who cooks for you, who cooks for you all?"

That voice didn't fool me. Somehow, some way everyone was in the know about last night's fiasco, includin' Daddy. Bobby began the funny puns, also known as *paronomasias* (Ronald taught me that): "Thanks for owl you do, Uncle Harold."

"Boys, *owl* was everything last night?"

"Let's just say it was a *hoot*!" bellowed Dean.

"*Whoo* stayed up the latest?"

"Duane did," Karen responded as Duane jumped down from the truck. "He's quite the night *owl*!"

"Karen, that was *fowl*," Duane replied. "*Owl* get you for that one!"

"Why did you sleep in the truck, Duane?"

"Don't you know birds of a feather *hoot* together! Besides, the girls didn't want to be *owl* by themselves!"

Standin' on the truck bed, I added, "*Owl* always be there if you need me—*owl* night long!"

Arms extended, I flew like a fowl into my father's arms. Daddy chuckled. "Look *whoo's* talking."

Mr. Know-It-All concluded the nonsense with, "*Hooray!* We had a *hoot—owl* of us!"

We broke camp and kept our eyes peeled on our way home for you-know-whoo!!!

Shoes for Thought!

Fiddlesticks and gumdrop bars! One look at the clock and I saw my nap had lasted three hours! One look on my pillow revealed Billy Bob the BedBug. Talkin' a mile a minute to catch him up on what he'd missed, I stopped when I realized it was all about me. So I asked, "What have you been up to?"

"You're not the only one who has cousins. Good thing I decided to go to my bedbug family reunion at the last minute. It was scary but I stepped up to the plate."

"What happened?"

"Everything was picture perfect until a one-eyed, one-horned flying blue-bug insect eater showed up. You've always challenged me to have courage! So I became a Superbug, mustered up some courage and saved the day!"

Horsefeathers! Billy Bob's story smelled a little fishy. Fortunately the phone rang, drawin' my attention away to Daddy's one-sided conversation. "How old is she? How many hands? Is she broke? What color? Is she gentle? Does she have shoes?"

Turnin' to Billy Bob, I saw his antenna raised; he whispered, "No need to explain. I've got bugs in all kinds of places. Gotta fly, we'll catch up later!"

Momma hollered, "Time to eat!"

Diane—sweet, not sulky—had helped the homemakers fix lunch. Grandma got the *heebie-jeebies* as we three siblings shared our spooky shenanigan stories. *Miss Hawkephant* was relieved she didn't spend the night. The undercover angel, elated to see I had retrieved her gloves, was more interested in lessons learned than all the tomfoolery. So I shared.

Scared Silly Secret Poem

Scared silly secret so simple and true,
Parents protect, guard and watch over you.
"Stop, look and listen" is an absolute must,
Family and parents are the ones you can trust.

A fledging is nudged right out of its nest,
The parents don't want to, but they know what is best.
Camp out, ride a bike, catch a fish, hook a worm.
They're scary at first, but we all live and learn.

Hanging by a rung, at the end of your rope,
Turn to family and friends for faith, love and hope.
When you're in a pickle or get in a bind,
Put trust in your family to have peace of mind.

Scared silly secret is simple and true,
It's not what's on the outside but inside of you.
Have courage, seek wisdom, know that you know,
Your family's behind you wherever you go!

Grandma beamed, as only angels can, then handed each one of us a box. Acceptin' mine, I said, "Grandma, may I share somethin'? Listen closely, I may never say this again. My brothers are better than any superheroes! Duane, like a bumblebee, you defended 'n' protected me from somethin' that gives you the *heebie-jeebies*—flyin' objects! You *can* always be trusted. Ronald backed us up, knowin' just what to do to scare that fowl owl away."

Mother chimed in. "Daddy and I commend you on trusting your brothers to protect you. It's difficult for siblings to get along, but when things get tough, always, always count on family." She tapped my box: "Open your surprise."

"Penny loafers!"

Positionin' the pennies, I put them on. Then Grandma and I exchanged a hug, and I ran in place. "Thanks, Grandma, for helpin' me know the difference between head knowledge and heart knowledge."

She smiled. "Wherever you go, whatever you do, you can trust someone is watching over you."

"Good news!" Duane added. "It's not the owl!"

"Speaking of owls," Daddy commented, "Ronald, I am so proud of how you kept a watchful *eye* on everyone. Use this *wisely*!"

Ronald, speechless for once, was now the proud owner of the one and only one-eyed, one-horned flyin' purple people eater costume. Daddy bragged, "Ronald never ceases to amaze us with all the head knowledge his brain holds. You encourage all of us to read more."

Diane chimed in. "'Cause if you weed a wot you know a wot!"

How can we not love the *Hawkephant?*

Proud of Duane and sensitive to her mother, Momma acknowledged, "Maybe Ronda's nice little ponytail coming out the top of her head looked to that owl like a *you-know-what*! So it swooped down on the ponytail, thinking it was lunch! But you showed up right on time, saved the day and became a hero—like Mighty *You-know-who* or Superman—a protector and defender."

"Cheesy pizza!" Runnin' around in circles, modelin' his new embroidered shirt and cape complete with his personalized inscription, Duane boasted, "I'm *SuperDuane*!"

I said, "Momma's right. If it weren't for you, those owls' talons could have done a lot more than messed up my hair."

"Wat 'bout me?"

Daddy pulled *Miss Hawkephant* away from the table, stretched out her legs and balanced a honey bear on her knees, "You are as sweet..."

"...as bee's knees!"

A homemade crown placed on her head, *Queen Bee* was all smiles and no sulks. Truth be known, I can't wait until Diane is old enough to join in all the fun. It's not always easy beeein' the baby in the family. Although *Queen Bees* do get out of work.

The rest of us worker bees finished chores. Daddy gave the thumbs-up sign as Ronald headed to the back cornfield to plow, and then winked at me as he left for the cattle auction. **Fiddlesticks and gumdrop bars!** Could it be? Sometimes at the auction there's more than cattle bein' sold. And what was that phone call all about?

Exhausted, I took an afternoon nap.

Woken up again by a tap on the shoulder, I saw Duane's face with "somethin' *was wrong*" written all over it. Grabbin' my hand, SuperDuane told me to trust him as we rushed down the stairs, flew out the door, ran down the sidewalk, past the garage then past the milk house. Out of the corner of my eye, I observed the cattle truck swayin' back 'n' forth. Could it be? I was curious. Duane wouldn't let me stop. This *must* be important.

All I knew is that Duane, from his bedroom window, had seen somethin' horrific happen in the back cornfield. Sprintin' past the barn, the feedlot, the shed, over the bridge and down the lane, we finally arrived.

What a disaster!
What a mess!
What a catastrophe!

We dared not get too close to the action. Physically Ronald looked fine but he was visibly shaken. Daddy, holdin' on to a big stick, made Ronald get down off the tractor. As they stood side by side, you could tell even from a distance, Ronald was gettin' quite an earful.

And by the look of things it spelled one word:

T - R - O - U - B - L - E!!!

To find out what happens,
you'll *hafta* read the next book!

*Keep your eyes peeled
and look for the sunflowers!
Every full illustration in this book
has a sunflower hidden in the page.*

Bobwhite
(Bobwhite)

choo-choo
(Possum)

Screech
(Bats)

peeper ribbit
(Tree Frog)

eek eek eek
(Mouse)

OooLuLLLu
(Turkey)

Hoo Hoo Hoo
Hoo Hoo Hoo
hooooo-ah
(Barred Owl)

(Skunk)
hiss, squeal, screech, whine,
whimper, stomp

chirp
(Crickets)

whinny
(Screech Owl)

(Katydid)
Katydid, katy-didn't

whoop-whoop
(Raccoon)

skreek
(Rat)

Whip-poor-will
(Whippoorwill)

(Flying Squirrel)
Tseep

ow wow wow wow
(Fox)

OUTDOOR-BAKED PINEAPPLE
UPSIDE-DOWN CAKE

20-ounce can crushed pineapple (drained)
¼ C. butter
½ C. brown sugar (packed firmly)
1 ½ package pound cake mix
3 large eggs — 1¼ C. milk

Line dutch oven with aluminum foil. Place oven on heat, level it and melt the butter on the oven. When melted, add brown sugar then crushed pineapple that has been drained. While butter is melting, mix the cake according to package directions. Pour the batter over the glaze and put lid on pan.

Bake in coals about 25 minutes, until golden brown, or until a toothpick, inserted near the middle, comes out clean. Lift out of pan by edges of aluminum foil; invert onto plate. Remove from foil. Serves 12.

LAYERED JELL-O SALAD

1 can crushed pineapple
¼ C. sugar
1 envelope plain gelatin
8 ounces Philadelphia cream cheese
½ pint whipping cream
2 3-ounce packages of red Jell-O

Add ¼ cup sugar to the crushed pineapple. Bring to boil and cook five minutes. Remove from stove and add plain gelatin which has been dissolved in ½ cup cold water. Put in large casserole dish (13x9½) to set. Soften cheese with a little milk and add to whipped cream.
Place over pineapple after it has set. Chill until firm. Prepare red Jell-O; let it cool till it is ready to gel, and spread on top. Refrigerate and serve chilled.

Harold Eugene Friend
"Daddy"

Jean Vivian Friend
"Momma"

"Down on Friendly Acres,"
painted by Grandma Brombaugh's sister, Pauline

Uncle Robert, Aunt Erta,
and cousin Bobby

Uncle Herman and
Aunt Pauline

Friend Family Cousins
"Pranks for the memories!"

Harold Friend's Sulky Barn
"Daddy's pride and joy!"

Sgt. Harold Eugene Friend
"Army Horse"

Harold Eugene Friend
"Quite the joker!"

Friendly Acres Woods
"S'mores — coming right up!"

Friendly Acres Milk House
"Run, run as fast
as you can!"

Owl Fowl
"A barred owl
to be exact!"

125

Besides Grandma Brombaugh,
What Do Other People Say About Trustworthiness?

"Few things help an individual more than to place responsibility upon him, and to let him know that you trust him." – Booker T. Washington

"To be trusted is a greater compliment than to be loved." – George MacDonald

"Anyone who doesn't take truth seriously in small matters cannot be trusted in large ones either." – Albert Einstein

"We must not promise what we ought not, lest we be called on to perform what we cannot." – Abraham Lincoln

"Trust is the glue of life. It's the most essential ingredient in effective communication. It's the foundational principle that holds all relationships." – Stephen R. Covey

"Trust takes years to build, seconds to break, and forever to repair." – Unknown

"Trust is like an eraser; it gets smaller and smaller after every mistake." – Unknown

According to Noah . . .

Trustworthy: worthy of confidence, dependable

Trustworthiness: worthiness as the recipient of another's trust or confidence

About the Author

Ronda Friend is an author, professional storyteller and founder of Sunflower Seeds Press, whose mission is reaching children's hearts and minds by sowing seeds of a different kind.

P.U. You Stink is Ronda's debut picture book in a series entitled *Wild and Wacky Animal Tales*. Future titles include *Waddle I Do Without You* (friendship) and *Monkey See, Monkey Do!* (obedience).

R. Friend's beloved chapter series—*Down on Friendly Acres*—is a nostalgic look back at life in the '60s. Woven into her true tall tales, playful poetry, catchy lyrics and melodic melodies are valuable life lessons on kindness, forgiveness, patience, perseverance and honesty.

Ronda holds a B. A. degree in education and a minor in music. She lives in Franklin, Tennessee, and is very happily married to her best friend, Bill. They are blessed with two grown children, Jeremy (his wife, Joy, along with granddaughter, Eva Jean) and Stephanie. There are many things in this world to be grateful for, but Ronda sums it all up with the three F's—family, faith and friends.

RondaFriend.com (booking information available)
SunflowerSeedsPress.com (read sample chapters from other books)
DownOnFriendlyAcres.com (children's website)

Remember . . .

Grandma Brombaugh says,

"One can't buy trust—trust is earned.

Earning trust requires learning from your mistakes.

It takes time but it's well worth the wait!"